For Isabella, Thomas, and Anna—three brave,
beautiful butterflies. —A. S.

I would like to dedicate this book to my Dad (Yuanhuang Xie) and
my mom (Yan Chen) —D. C.

STERLING CHILDREN'S BOOKS
New York

An Imprint of Sterling Publishing Co., Inc.
1166 Avenue of the Americas
New York, NY 10036

ISBN 978-1-4549-2119-6

Distributed in Canada by Sterling Publishing Co., Inc.
c/o Canadian Manda Group, 664 Annette Street
Toronto, Ontario M6S 2C8, Canada
Distributed in the United Kingdom by GMC Distribution Services
Castle Place, 166 High Street, Lewes, East Sussex BN7 1XU, England
Distributed in Australia by NewSouth Books
University of New South Wales, Sydney, NSW 2052, Australia

For information about custom editions, special sales, and premium
and corporate purchases, please contact Sterling Special Sales
at 800-805-5489 or specialsales@sterlingpublishing.com.

Manufactured in United States of America

Lot #:
2 4 6 8 10 9 7 5 3
08/19

sterlingpublishing.com

Cover and interior design by Irene Vandervoort

A month before school, Rosie picked out her very first backpack.

It was covered with flowers, and she loved it with all her heart.

She paraded around proudly. "Don't worry," she told her sister, Emily. "Someday you'll be big enough to go to school like me."

Rosie practiced raising her hand, writing her letters,
and saying her teacher's name.
She couldn't wait to start school.

But the night before her first day, Rosie
couldn't sleep.

In the morning, her belly hurt.

She didn't touch her chocolate chip pancakes.

"Maybe I'd better stay home," said Rosie. "I don't want Emily to be lonely."

"She'll be fine," said her mother. "And so will you."

Rosie shuffled the pancakes around on her plate. "C'mon, sweetie," said her dad. "Time to go."

Rosie slowly pulled on her backpack. "I don't feel well," she said. "You just have butterflies in your belly," said her mother, hugging her tight. "Butterflies?" asked Rosie.

That's when the bus pulled up.

"I love you," said her mom.

"Have fun!" called her dad.

Rosie stared nervously out the window.

Soon, a girl sat down next to her.

"I'm Violet," she said. "What's your name?"

"Rosie."

As she spoke, a butterfly flew from her mouth.

Rosie clapped both hands over her face.

"Are you okay?"

Rosie nodded.

"I have Mrs.
Mancini," said Violet.

"Me, too!" said Rosie.

The words tumbled out on two silver butterflies.

Rosie watched them flutter down the aisle.

Violet didn't seem to notice.

"Welcome," said Mrs. Mancini as the girls entered the classroom. "Hang up your backpacks, then meet me on the rainbow rug."

Everyone fidgeted in a circle.
"Let's get to know each other," said Mrs. Mancini. "I'll go first. I have a golden retriever named Barney. I love chocolate cake, and I'm terrified of spiders."

Violet went next.

"I'm allergic to dogs," she said. "And sometimes to my brother, Alex."

"This summer I rode a train for the first time," said Jay.

"I want to be an astronaut when I grow up," said Alison.

The butterflies built up as Rosie waited for her turn.

Suddenly, all eyes were on her.

Rosie took a deep breath.

"I have a baby sister named Emily,"
she said.

Three butterflies flitted into the air.

"I love to sing and play soccer. I wish I
had a freezer in my room so I could eat ice
cream whenever I want."

The class laughed.
Rosie's belly felt a little better.

After that, Rosie sat at the art table.

She painted a flower on a giant easel.

She made one for Violet, too.

Then they helped Jay build a train out of blocks.

From time to time, butterflies rumbled in Rosie's belly.

Occasionally, one or two slipped out.

But by recess, she could barely feel them anymore.

Rosie dashed onto the playground.

"You're it!" she called.

Everyone raced around playing tag.

But one girl stood alone under the oak tree.

She held her hands on her belly.
Rosie walked over to her.

"Wanna play?" she asked.

The girl nodded.

"I'm Rosie. What's your name?"

"Isabella."

As she answered, butterfly after butterfly soared into the sky.

Isabella looked up, amazed.

"Feel better?" asked Rosie.

"Much," said Isabella.

At the end of the
day, Rosie waved goodbye
to her friends.

She ran off the bus and
leapt into her mother's arms.
"School is so fun," she
said. "Violet has a flower name
like me, and Jay built a train
out of blocks, and Isabella had
butterflies, too!"

Butterflies ON THE
First Day of School

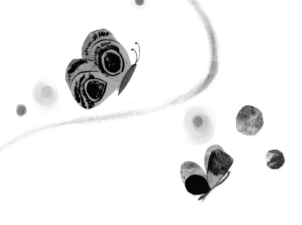

By ANNIE SILVESTRO
Illustrated by DREAM CHEN

STERLING CHILDREN'S BOOKS
New York

Her mother smiled.

"I can't wait to hear all about it," she said.

The words floated out on a shimmering butterfly's wings.